DRAGONS
of New Orleans

Story by Bruce Dear • Illustrated by Samantha Smith

Dragons! Dragons!

Everywhere there are Dragons!

Across
the sea

and in
your tea

over the moon

And on a spoon

But a sleeping dragon in your home?

Are you looking behind the bed?

Ah silly! It's all in your head.

Dragons! Dragons!

Everywhere there are Dragons!

Red
Dragons

Blue
Dragons

Old
Dragons

Cold Dragons

Baby Dragons

with Mama Dragons

A dragon swinging in an oak

Or fishing from a boat.

But a dragon swimming
in a swamp?

yikes! They have alligators... probably not.

you can have a dragon as a pet...

Or see one zooming in a jet.

And
if
you
find
20 Dragons
dancing in
time...

That's
what
they
call
a second
line!

There are **so** many dragons
They are **easy** to spot

But a hairy Dragon?

They have scales, I think not!

Dragons!
Dragons!
Everywhere there are Dragons!

There
are
Hungry
Dragons

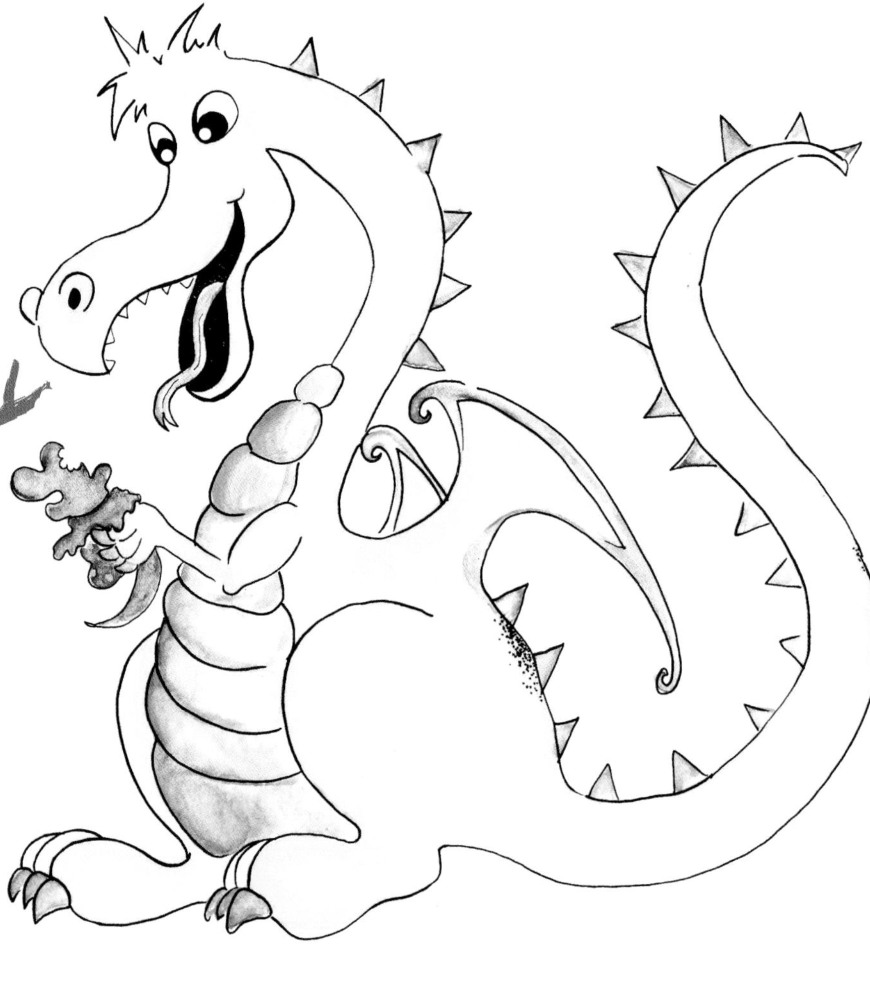

And

Fancy

Golden

Dragons

Dancing, Dizzy Dragons

and musical Dragons

Dragons flying in the sky while making a pecan pie.

A dragon
for a

T
E
A
C
H
E
R

Or even as a preacher...

There are
many things
Dragons can do

The only question is...

what kind of Dragon are you?

A division of Mind to Marketplace for more info visit: Mindtomarketplace.com

Credits:

Written by: Bruce Dear
Illustrations by: Samantha Smith
Book Design by: Mósa Tanksley

First Edition
CIP data for this book is available from the Library of Congress

ISBN 978-1-48358-657-1

Dedicated to our children who know the importance of Dragons... long may it be so.